THE USBORNE BOOK OF PRINTING

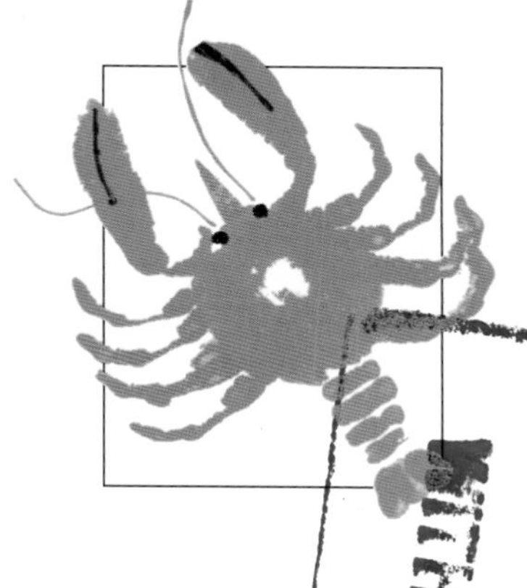

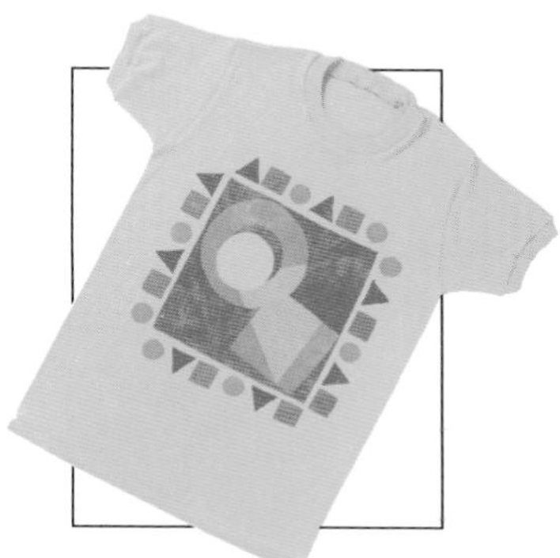

Ray Gibson

Edited by Fiona Watt
Designed by Mary Cartwright and Vicki Groombridge
Illustrated by John Woodcock · Photographs by Howard Allman
Series editor: Cheryl Evans

Contents

Hints and tips	2	Sun, moon and stars	18
Hand and finger prints	4	Hearts and squares	20
Vegetable flowers	6	Leaves, corks and bottle tops	22
Sponge print plates	8	Rubber stamps	24
Juggling frogs	10	Flour paste batik	26
Roller print T-shirt	12	Lots more prints	28
Marbled paper	14	Templates	30
Penguin potato prints	16	Cushions and stitches	32

Hints and tips

It's a good idea to read through these two pages before you start to print. You'll find lots of handy hints which will help you to get good results. Make sure that you always cover the place where you are working with lots of newspaper. You'll also need to cover a place to dry your prints. Wear something to protect your clothes so that they don't get messy.

Paints

You can use any water-based paints for the projects in this book. If you want to print on fabric use either fabric paint or liquid acrylic. How dark or light the paper or fabric is will affect the shade of your print, so test the paint on a scrap before you begin.

Use paper which will not wrinkle or tear when you print on it. Try using different kinds of paper, such as textured paper, plain giftwrap or brown paper.

Red paint may turn brown on blue paper or fabric.

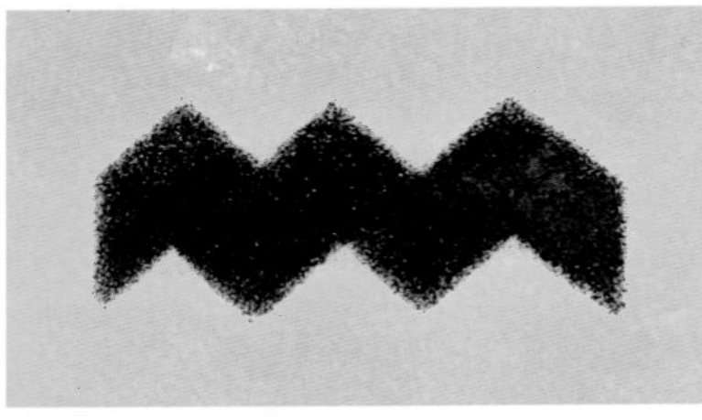

Blue paint may turn dull and greenish if you print on yellow.

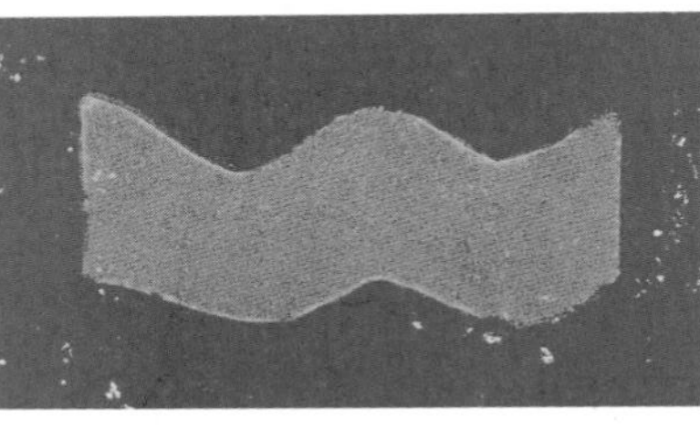

Light shades don't always show up well on dark surfaces.

Use a small decorator's or artist's paintbrush to apply paint to delicate things, like leaves, which you can't easily press onto a printing pad.

Printing pad

A printing pad is useful for putting paint onto the thing you are printing with. You can make one from a sponge cleaning cloth or a thick piece of cotton or wool fabric.

Use the back of the spoon to spread the paint evenly over the sponge.

Put the cloth or fabric onto newspaper. Spread paint on with an old spoon or a piece of cardboard. Press the thing you are printing with into the paint so that it is evenly covered.

Small decorator's paintbrush

Artist's brush

Brown paper

Patterned paper

Tissue paper

Bright paper

Textured paper

Bottle tops and jar lids

Things to print with

All the projects in this book use things for printing which you may have around your home. Look for objects with unusual shapes or patterns on them.

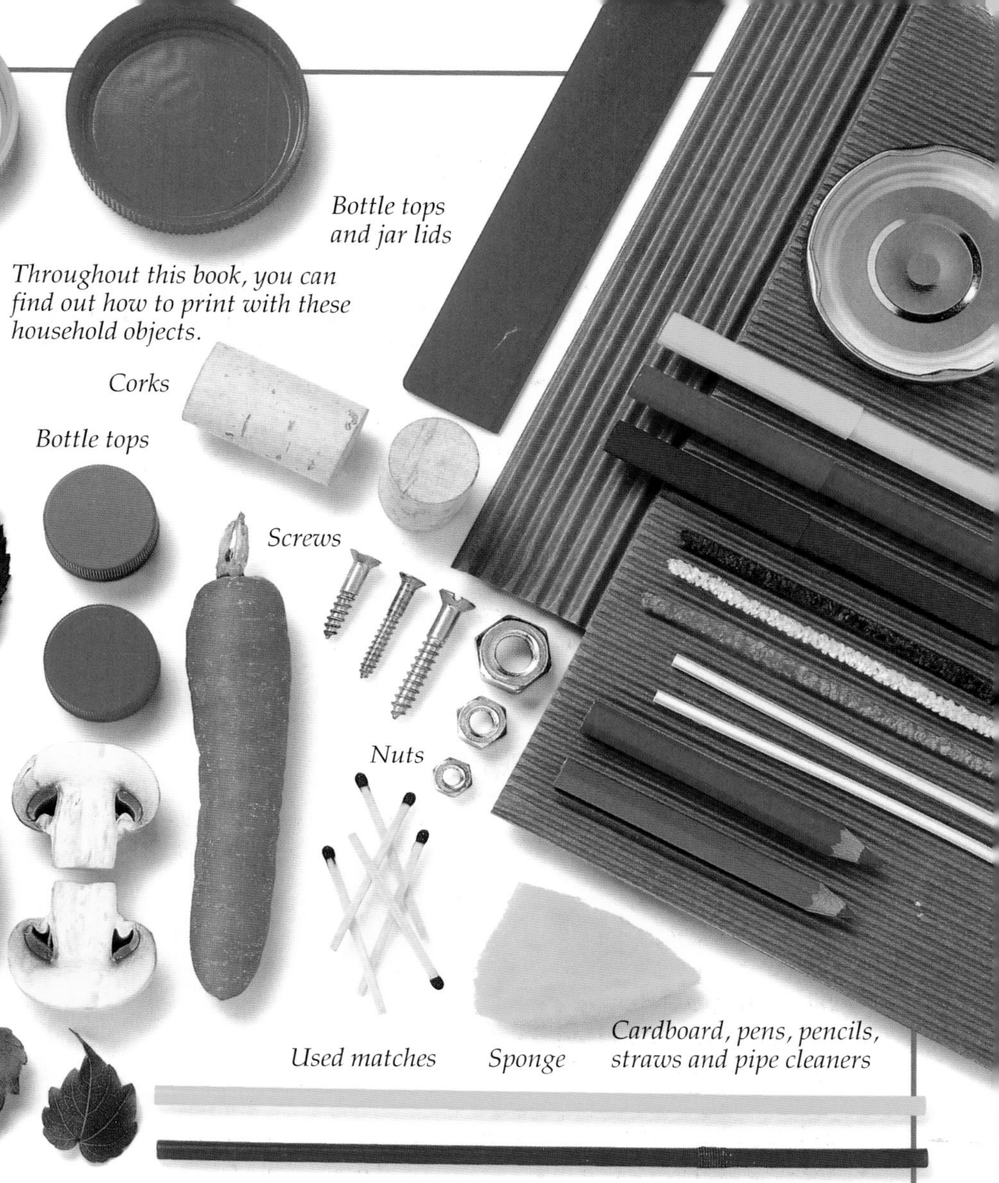

Throughout this book, you can find out how to print with these household objects.

Corks

Bottle tops

Screws

Nuts

Leaves and vegetables

Used matches

Sponge

Cardboard, pens, pencils, straws and pipe cleaners

Sponge cleaning cloth

Printing with vegetables

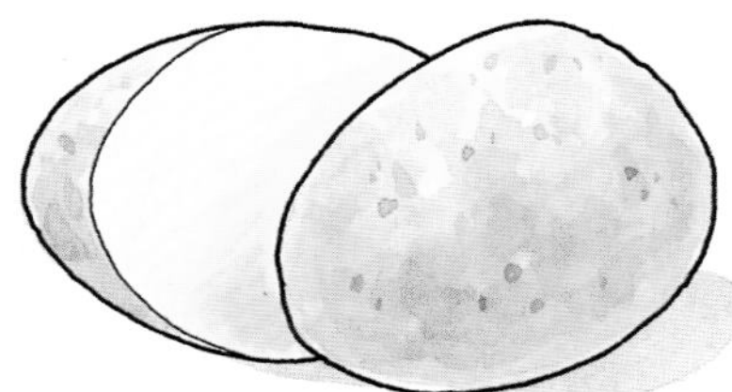

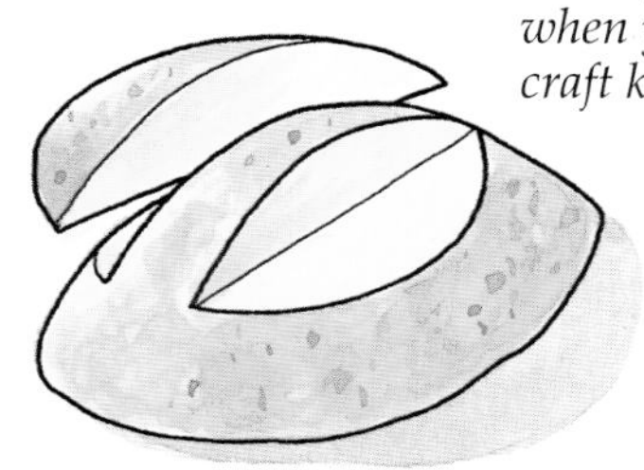

Be very careful when you use a craft knife.

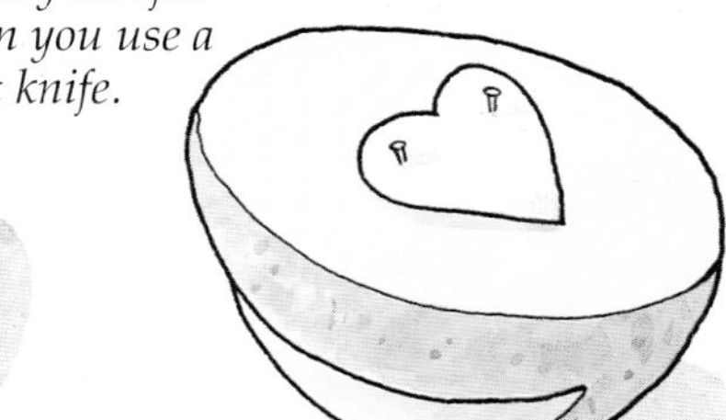

If you print with a potato or another 'round' vegetable, it's a good idea to cut a handle in the back so that it's easy to hold. Cut the vegetable in half.

Make two cuts along the top with a craft knife 2cm ($\frac{3}{4}$in) apart. Then, slice in from the sides and remove the wedges which you have cut.

You can cut around a template so that you get a neat shape to print. Draw or trace it onto thin paper then push in pins to hold it while you cut.

Hand and finger prints

It's best to do this print near a sink full of warm water as you'll have to wash your hands often. Dry them on an old cloth after washing them. **You will need:** several shades of ready-mix paint; water; sponge cloth for a printing pad (see page 2); small decorator's paintbrush; newspaper; thin cardboard or an old postcard; a large piece of thick paper.

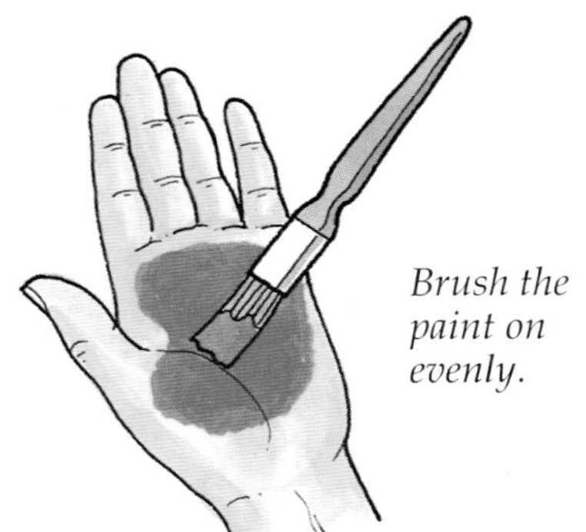

Brush the paint on evenly.

1. Mix red paint with a little water to thin it. Use the paintbrush to paint the palm of your left hand.

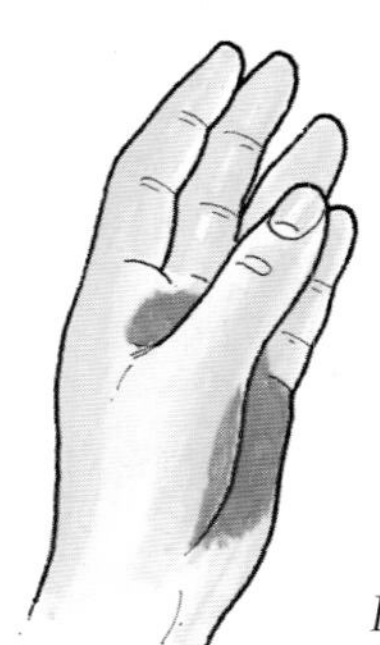

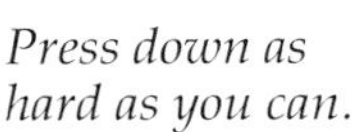

Press down as hard as you can.

2. Press your hand onto the paper to print the main part of the body. Hold the paper as you lift your hand.

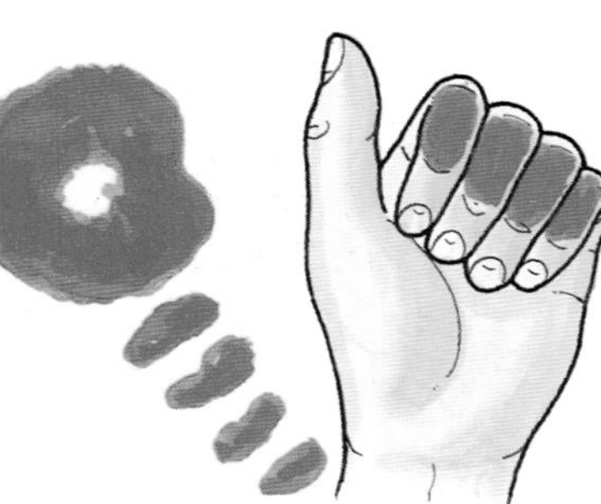

3. Press the front of a clenched fist onto red paint on a sponge cloth. Turn your hand sideways and print a tail.

4. To print the end of the tail, press your thumb onto the sponge cloth, then do three overlapping prints.

Turn the paper around.

Print this claw with your right hand.

5. Clench your right fist and press into paint. Print a big claw on the right. Do the left claw with your left hand.

Print the left legs with your left hand.

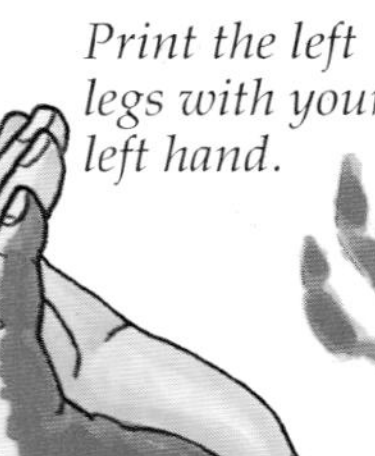

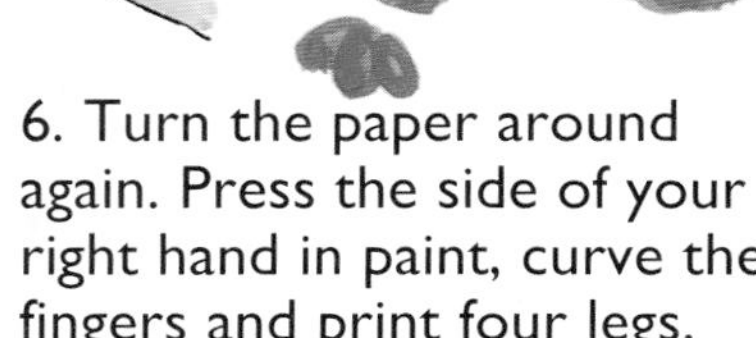

6. Turn the paper around again. Press the side of your right hand in paint, curve the fingers and print four legs.

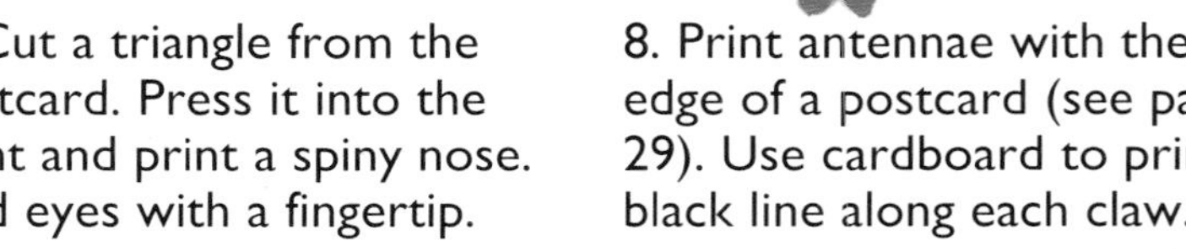

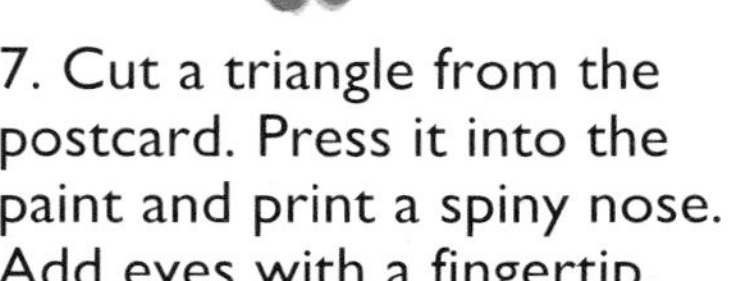

7. Cut a triangle from the postcard. Press it into the paint and print a spiny nose. Add eyes with a fingertip.

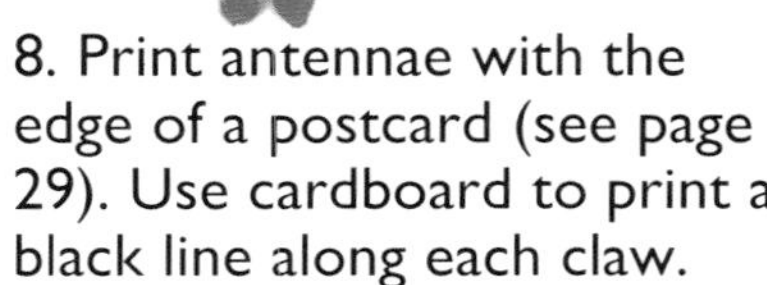

8. Print antennae with the edge of a postcard (see page 29). Use cardboard to print a black line along each claw.

Print a prawn

1. Print a pink body with the side of your fist (see step 5 of the lobster).

2. Add a black eye with a fingertip. Print pink 'feelers' with a cardboard edge.

3. Print several legs under the body with the bent edge of some cardboard.

For a sea anemone, print a curved edge of cardboard again and again in circular pattern.

Print a fan-shaped shell by dipping the edge of cardboard into different paints. Press it onto the paper and twist it around.

Print seaweed with the edge of cardboard pressed into two shades of paint.

Vegetable flowers

The flowers on these pages are printed with different vegetables.

You will need: ready-mix paints or acrylic paints; small decorator's paintbrush; cardboard; kitchen paper towels; newspaper; sharp knife; sponge cleaning cloth; clean scrap of paper; button mushrooms; large carrot; small potato; fresh leaves.

Poppy

Be very careful as you cut.

1. Cut the top off the carrot with one clean slice. Very carefully, make several cuts 1.5cm (½in) deep across the end.

2. Stand the carrot on a paper towel for a minute or so. Paint the cut end of the carrot with black paint, then press it firmly on your paper.

Overlap the prints.

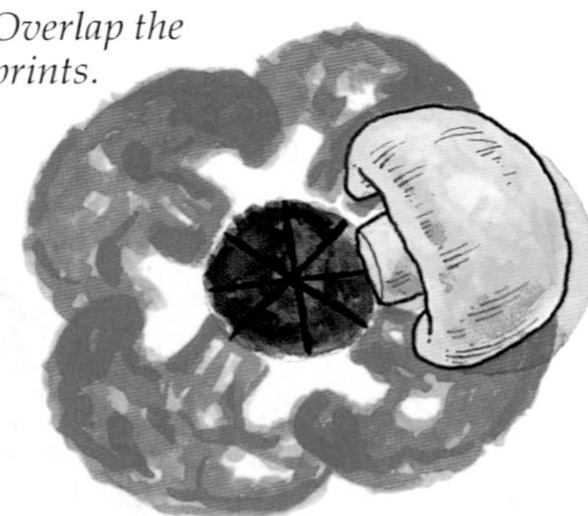

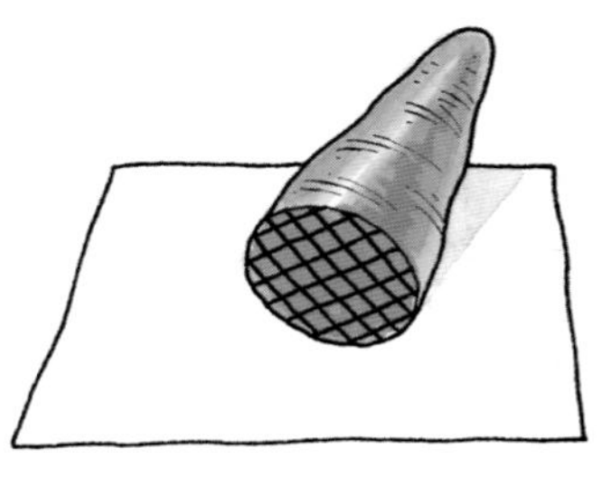

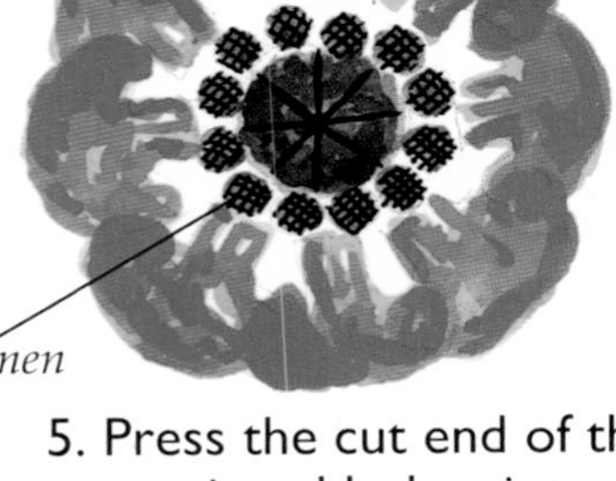

Stamen

3. Cut the mushroom in half. Blot it on a paper towel, then paint with red. Print it at the top, bottom and the sides, then in the spaces in between.

4. For the stamens, cut 2½cm (1in) piece of carrot from the pointed end. Very carefully make lots of criss-cross cuts across it. Blot it well.

5. Press the cut end of the carrot into black paint and print shapes all around the middle of the poppy. Overlap the prints a little.

Find out on page 22 how to do a leaf print.

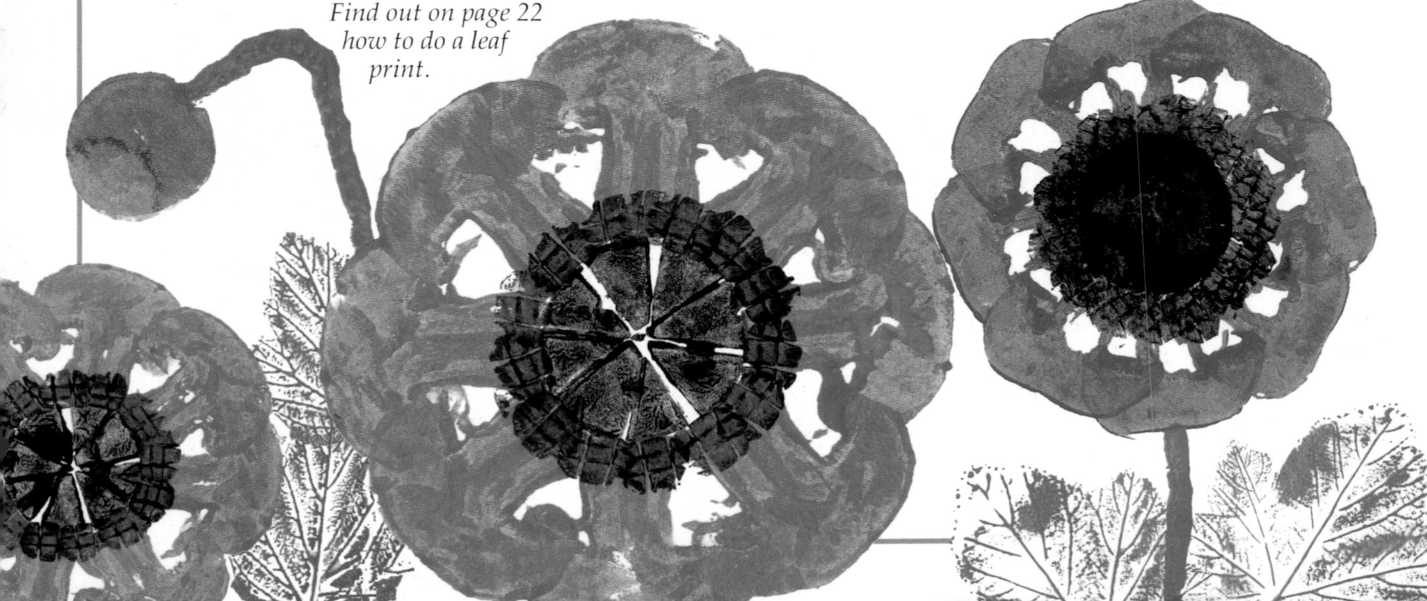

Fold the sponge cloth to print a bent stem.

6. For a half-open bud, print two overlapping petals with the mushroom. Add a stalk with the edge of a piece of sponge cloth (see page 8).

7. For a closed bud, cut across the big piece of carrot. Paint the end green and add a tiny bit of red as well. Print the stalk with sponge cloth.

Sunflower

For the middle of the flower, slice a cut potato with criss-cross cuts to make diamond shapes. Blot it and print it with dark brown paint.

Cut a 5cm (2in) piece of carrot in half lengthways. Print eight bright yellow petals as for the poppy. Add darker yellow petals on top.

Anemones

Print this in the same way as the poppy, but don't make the cuts across the end of the carrot in step 1. Print it in red, blue, pink or purple.

Sponge print plates

You can buy a special kind of ceramic paint from many craft stores, which can be used to decorate china. You usually bake it in an oven to make it permanent, but you must not eat off these plates once you have decorated them.

You will need: white or pale shade of china plate; a piece of artificial sponge; two shades of ceramic paint; old jar lid; sponge cleaning cloth; ruler; scissors; masking tape.

Line up the strips at one end too.

1. Dip a piece of sponge into the lightest paint. Press it onto newspaper, then dab it lightly all over the plate. Leave it to dry.

2. Cut a piece of sponge cloth 17 x 4cm (7 x 1½in) and two pieces 15 x 3cm (6 x 1¼in). Lay them together, matching the top edges.

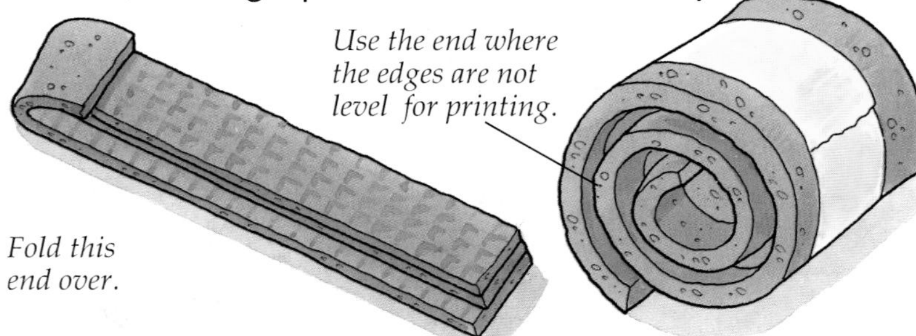

Use the end where the edges are not level for printing.

Fold this end over.

Don't press too hard.

3. Cut a piece of tape and lay it down so that it is ready to use. Fold the end of the long piece of sponge over the ends of the short pieces.

4. Roll up the sponges very neatly, but not too tightly. Keep the edges even. Wrap tape tightly around the sponge to secure it.

5. Pour a little ceramic paint onto a lid, then dip the end of the sponge into it. Try out your print on a piece of newspaper.

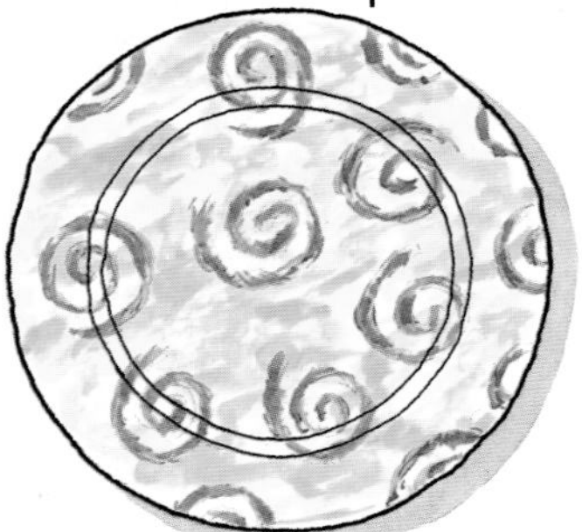

6. Print the shapes all over the sponged plate. When the paint has dried, follow the manufacturer's instructions for hardening it.

Bend a small piece of sponge to make a horseshoe shape.

Use the edge of a piece of sponge for straight lines.

Checked plates

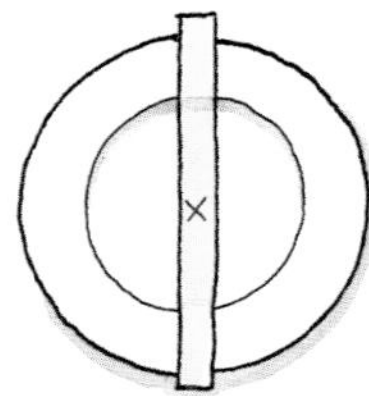

1. Lay a strip of tape across the plate. Mark the middle with a cross.

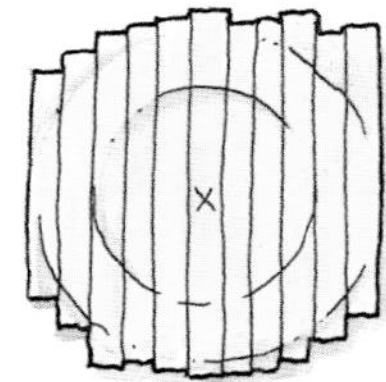

2. Add strips either side of the middle to cover the plate. Don't overlap them.

Sponge on the paint.

3. Peel off the tape either side of the middle then pull off every other one.

4. When dry, peel off the tape. Cross tape over the stripes. Repeat steps 1-3.

You can also print on paper or paper plates with sponge cloths.

You don't need to do a sponged pattern before you print.

If you print on a dark plate, the shade of your paint may change (see page 2). Test your paint on the bottom of the plate before you start.

These plates are for decoration only, you must not eat off them.

Bend the sponge in half for a V shape.

Juggling frogs

You will need: felt; pins; two shades of thread (one to match the felt); needle; old saucer; cork; greaseproof paper; four tablespoons of orange lentils; plastic spoon; ready-mix paint; big straw; household glue (PVA); pencil; used match; spoon; small plastic container; newspaper. For the printing paint, mix together two tablespoons of paint with a teaspoon of glue and a teaspoon of water.

Cut very carefully.

1. Trace the frog template on page 31 twice onto greaseproof paper. Pin each one onto some felt and cut them out. Remove the pins.

2. To print the frog's back, put a piece of scrap felt onto some newspaper. Spoon a little printing paint onto it and press the cork onto it.

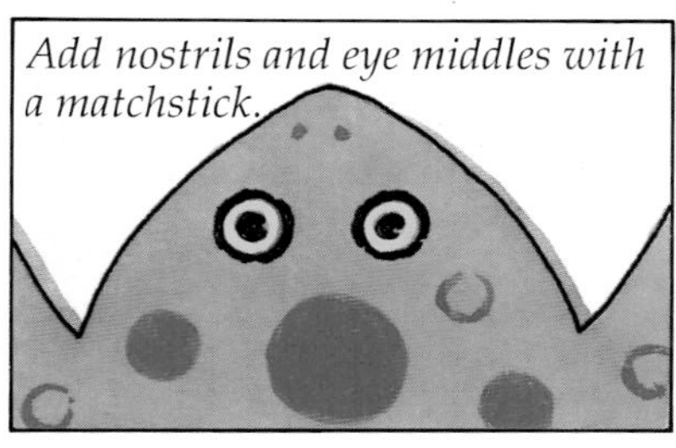

3. Print some large spots with the cork. Add smaller spots with the end of the pencil. Dip the straw into the paint and print lots of rings.

4. For the eyes, mix a little black paint with some glue and print them with a pencil end. When dry, print rings in yellow paint with a straw.

5. Dip the end of a straw in the paint and print some rings on the tummy of the other frog piece. Add tiny dots with a matchstick. Leave to dry.

Don't sew too close to the edge.

Leave the thread attached.

6. With the plain sides touching, pin the frog pieces together very neatly. Sew with long tacking stitches around the edge (see page 32).

7. Thread the needle. Tie the ends to make a double thread. Sew 3mm (1/8in) from the edge with backstitch (see page 32). Leave a gap at the bottom.

8. Remove the tacking stitches. Spoon some lentils into the head, knees and arms. Push them into the narrow parts with a pencil. Fill the body last.

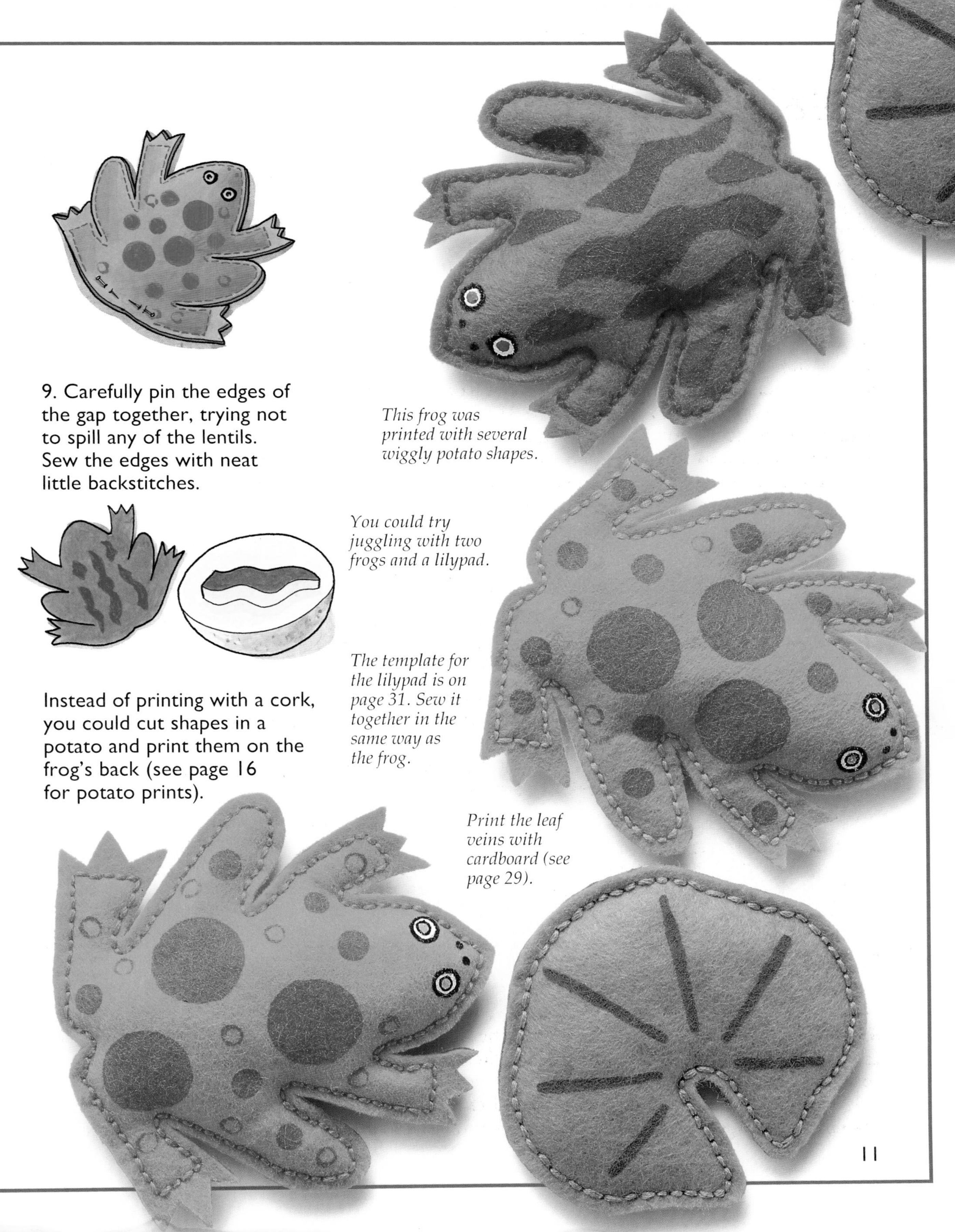

9. Carefully pin the edges of the gap together, trying not to spill any of the lentils. Sew the edges with neat little backstitches.

Instead of printing with a cork, you could cut shapes in a potato and print them on the frog's back (see page 16 for potato prints).

This frog was printed with several wiggly potato shapes.

You could try juggling with two frogs and a lilypad.

The template for the lilypad is on page 31. Sew it together in the same way as the frog.

Print the leaf veins with cardboard (see page 29).

Roller print T-shirt

You could do any of the prints in this book on a T-shirt, using fabric or acrylic paint. **You will need:** washed and ironed T-shirt; large piece of cardboard 1cm (½in) wider than your T-shirt; pins; ruler; masking tape; green, light blue and dark blue fabric paint or liquid acrylic paint; sponge cleaning cloth; black felt-tip pen; household paint roller; book-covering film; scissors; craft knife; newspaper.

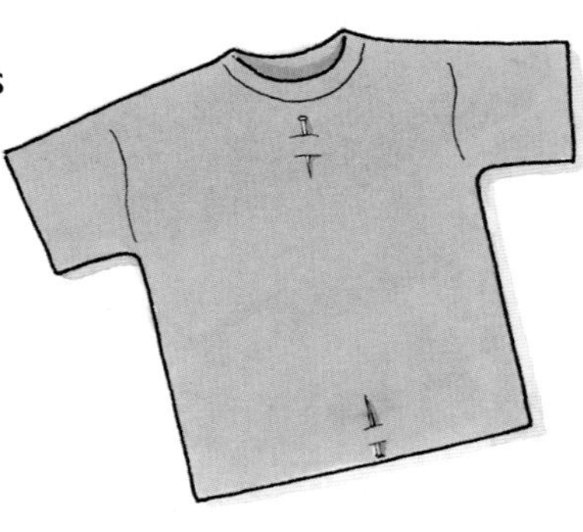

1. Fold the T-shirt exactly in half. Mark the middle with two pins, pushing them through the top layer only.

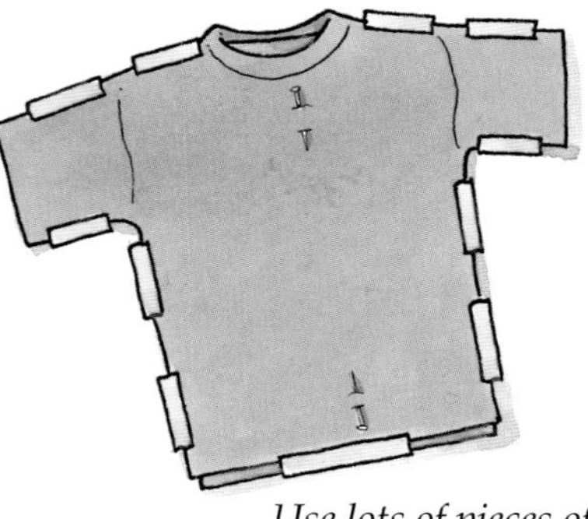

Use lots of pieces of tape around the edge.

2. Lay the T-shirt flat. Slide the cardboard inside and tape it onto a flat surface. Make sure that the front is smooth.

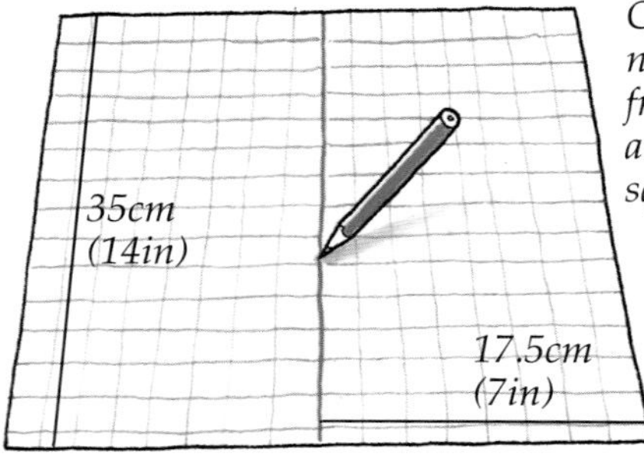

3. Draw a 35cm (14in) square onto the paper side of book-covering film. Cut it out, then rule a line down the middle.

Cut carefully as you need the frame and the square.

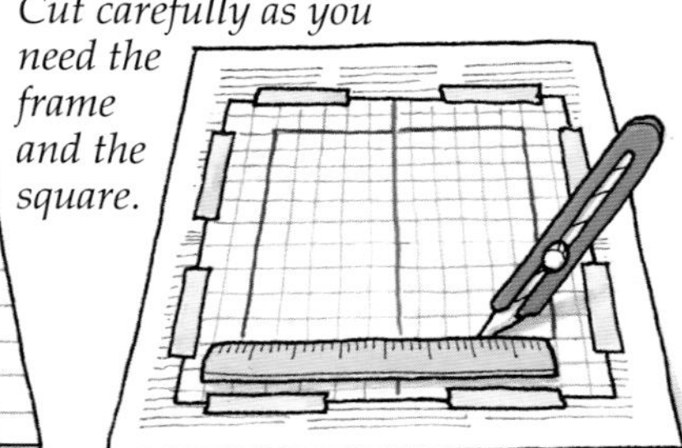

4. Make marks 7.5cm (3in) in from each side. Join them up to make a square. Tape it onto newspaper and cut it out.

Match the middle marks with the pins.

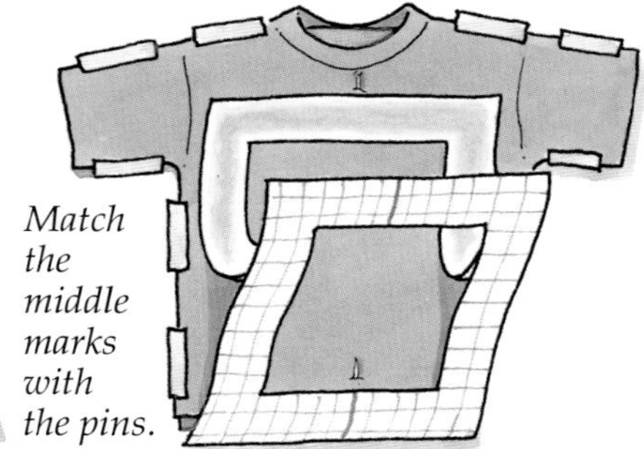

5. Peel the backing paper down from the top of the frame and press it on. Slowly peel off the rest, pressing it down firmly.

6. Tape pieces of scrap paper all around the square. Make sure that the paper overlaps the edges of the film.

7. Spread the palest paint over a sponge cloth. Run the roller across it then roll firmly over the square.

8. Draw several fish on the square which you cut out from the middle of the film. Cut them out carefully.

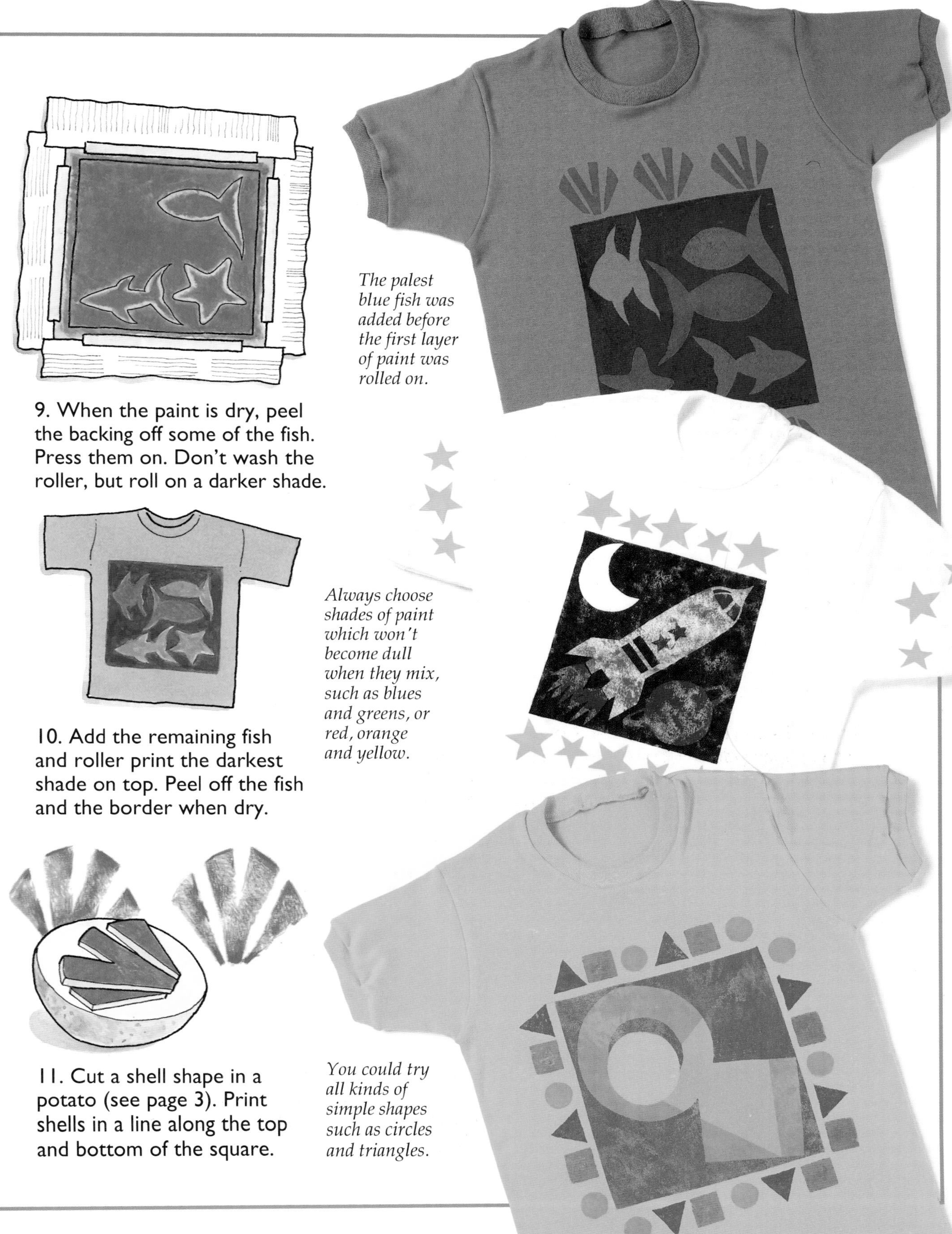

9. When the paint is dry, peel the backing off some of the fish. Press them on. Don't wash the roller, but roll on a darker shade.

10. Add the remaining fish and roller print the darkest shade on top. Peel off the fish and the border when dry.

11. Cut a shell shape in a potato (see page 3). Print shells in a line along the top and bottom of the square.

The palest blue fish was added before the first layer of paint was rolled on.

Always choose shades of paint which won't become dull when they mix, such as blues and greens, or red, orange and yellow.

You could try all kinds of simple shapes such as circles and triangles.

Marbled paper

Marbling is a kind of print you make by laying paper onto painty water then lifting it off. **You will need:** at least two shades of oil paint; a clean plastic container or jar for each shade of paint; roasting tray; paintbrush; paper kitchen towels; turpentine; kitchen foil; plastic spoons; lots of paper. Before you start, cover your work area with newspaper.

1. Line the roasting tray with two layers of foil to make it watertight. Fold the edges of the foil over the rim of the tray all the way around.

2. Trim the paper you are going to print on so that it fits into the tray without curling up at the edges. Fill the tray with cold water.

Mix two or three shades of paint.

Open a window before you mix the turpentine as it has a strong smell.

3. Squeeze some paint into a jar. Add a little turpentine and mix it in. Continue to add more turpentine until the mixture is like runny cream.

4. Using the tip of a paintbrush, drip the paint mixture all over the surface of the water. It will float on the top. Add other shades.

5. Slowly wiggle the end of the paintbrush in the water to break up the drops of paint. As you do this you'll make swirly patterns.

6. Hold the paper at each end and bend it in a curve. Lay the middle of the paper gently onto the surface of the water then lower the ends.

You could decorate cardboard folders and books with your marbled paper.

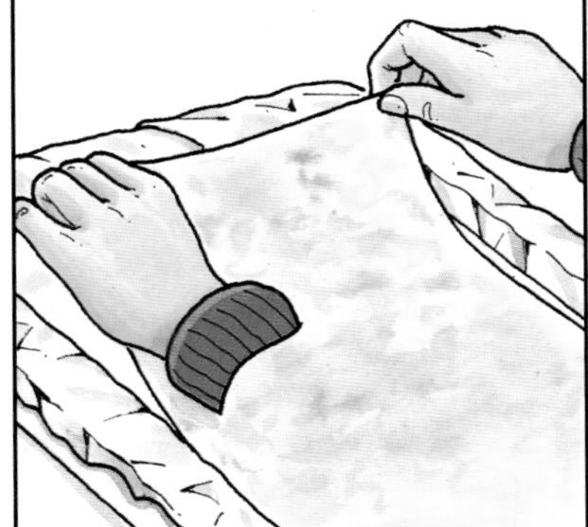

7. Pick up the corners at one end and lift it gently. Allow it to drip for a second or two, then lay it, paint-side up, on newspaper. Leave it to dry.

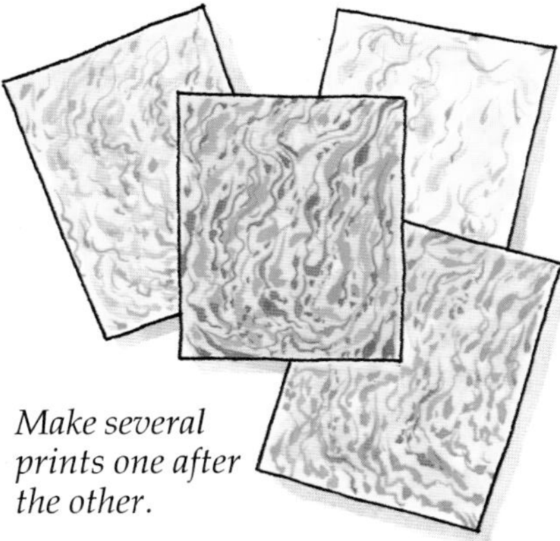

Make several prints one after the other.

8. You can make a paler print by laying another piece of paper on the water without adding more paint. Or, add more paint and print it again.

Cleaning up

Ask someone to help you to carry the tray and tip the painty water down an outside drain. Then, carefully fold in the sides of the foil without getting your hands messy and throw it away. Use a little turpentine on a paper towel to clean your hands, then wash them well in soapy water.

Penguin potato prints

Potatoes are some of the simplest things to print with as they are easy to cut. **You will need:** 1 large potato; sharp knife; craft knife; kitchen paper towels; newspaper; ready-mix paints; pencil; felt-tip pen; old saucer; paint brush; used matchstick; thick white paper; scissors, plastic foodwrap; small piece of sponge; two paper plates; glue; tape; strong thread.

Draw the lines at the narrowest end if there is one.

Be very careful as you cut.

1. Cut the potato from end to end with one clean cut. Blot the cut side on a paper towel. Draw lines to make a more pointed head shape.

2. Cut along the lines with the craft knife, making the cuts about 1cm (½in) deep. Then, slice in from the sides and remove the pieces.

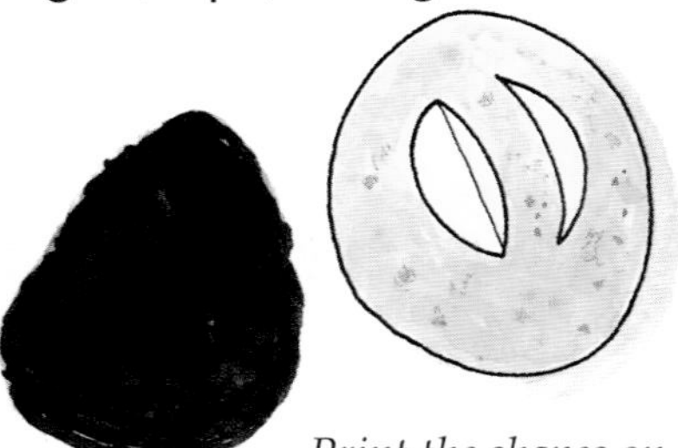

Print the shapes on the white paper.

Add yellow paint to one side before you print.

3. Cut a handle into the back (see page 3). Blot the flat side. Dip the potato into some black paint on a saucer. Print several body shapes.

4. Cut two 3cm (1¼in) wings, from the end of the spare half of the potato. Dip them in black paint and print one on either side of each body.

5. For the tummy, wash the body piece then trim it to an oval. Dip it in white paint and brush on some yellow. Print a tummy on each black shape.

6. Cut a triangle for the feet and one for a beak from the spare half potato. Print them in orange. Don't make all the beaks face the same way.

7. Use a pencil end to print a white eye on each penguin. Add a middle to each one. Cut around each penguin leaving a narrow white border.

These penguins and owls were taped one below another.

Print owls in the same way as the penguins, but use different shades of paint. Add V shapes with folded cardboard.

8. Paint some foodwrap with runny blue paint. Leave it for a minute then lay it, paint-side down over the back of a plate. Press lightly then peel it off.

9. Print orange paint onto the back of a plate with a sponge. Leave it to dry. Cut the blue plate into an iceberg shape. Glue it onto the orange plate.

10. Tape a thread onto the back of each penguin. Tape these to the plate at different heights. Tape on a loop at the top of the plate for hanging.

Sun, moon and stars

You could print this design on a piece of fabric and turn it into a wall hanging, a scarf, or a cushion cover (see page 32). You could also print on a pillowcase. If you do, cut a piece of cardboard the same size, cover one side of the cardboard with kitchen foil and slip it inside the pillowcase before you start.

You will need: washed and ironed cotton fabric; old scissors; two pieces of medium fine sandpaper; masking tape; soft pencil; ballpoint pen; greaseproof paper; paper clips; pins; small decorator's paintbrush; newspaper; old knife; pieces of scrap paper; several shades of fabric paints.

Use paper clips to attach the greaseproof paper.

1. Put greaseproof paper over the templates on page 30. Trace around all the shapes carefully with a soft pencil.

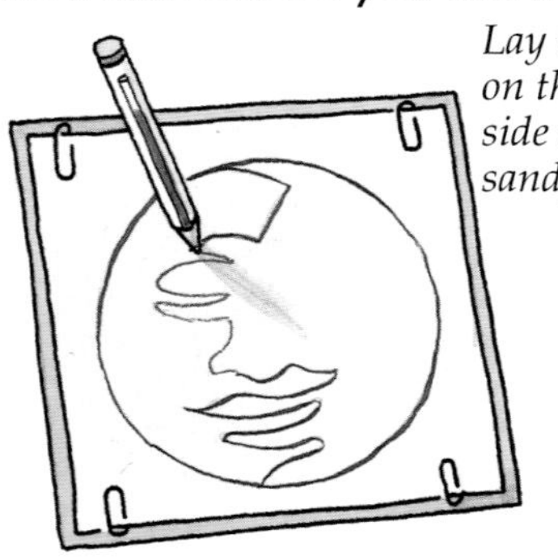

2. Lay the tracing pencil-side down on the sandpaper.Draw over the lines with the pen to transfer the shapes.

Lay the tracing on the smooth side of the sandpaper.

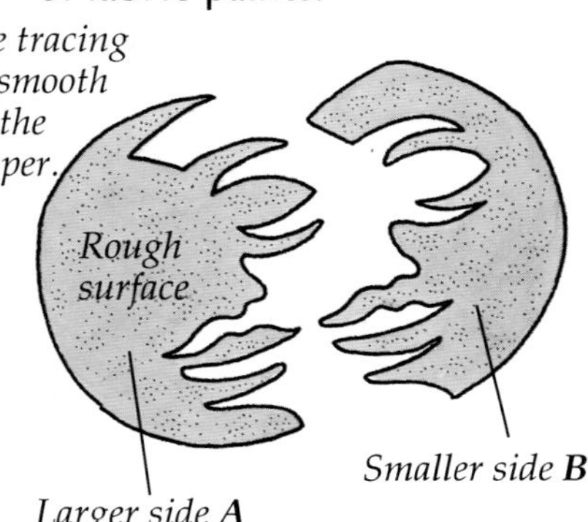

3. Cut around the circle outline first. Then, very carefully, cut along the middle line which makes the face.

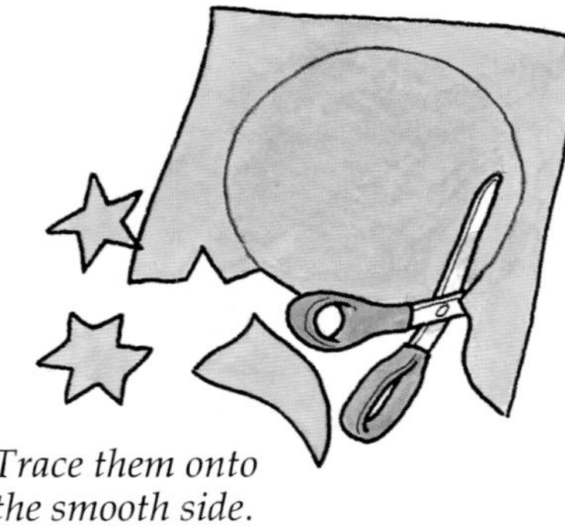

Trace them onto the smooth side.

4. Place the tracing on the other piece of sandpaper. Draw around the circle, stars and sun ray. Cut them out.

5. Mark the position of the shapes by laying the sandpaper circle on your fabric. Push pins in to mark their position.

If you print on a scarf, tape it flat onto cardboard first.

Lift the sandpaper circle off your fabric and brush paint onto the rough side.

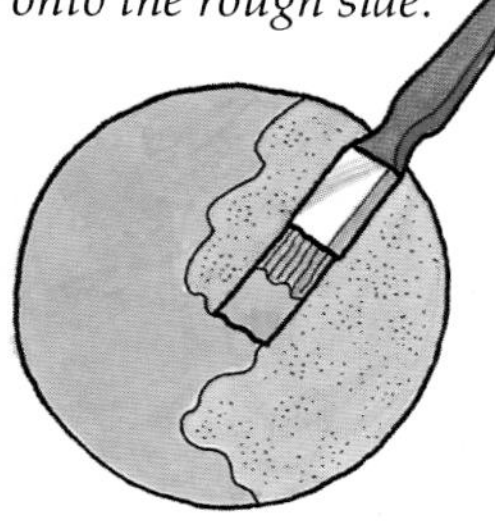

6. For the sun, brush the palest paint onto the rough side of the circle. Turn it over and place it between the pins.

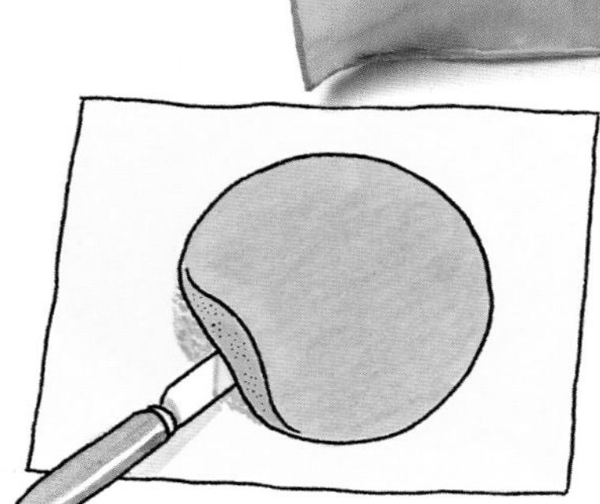

7. Lay a sheet of scrap paper over the circle. Press it down firmly all over. Lift up the edge with a knife and remove.

Match the curved edges.

8. Mix a slightly darker shade and paint it onto the rough side of **A**. Print it onto the right-hand side of the circle.

9. Paint the sun ray and print it at the top of the face. Repeat at the bottom and then at each side.

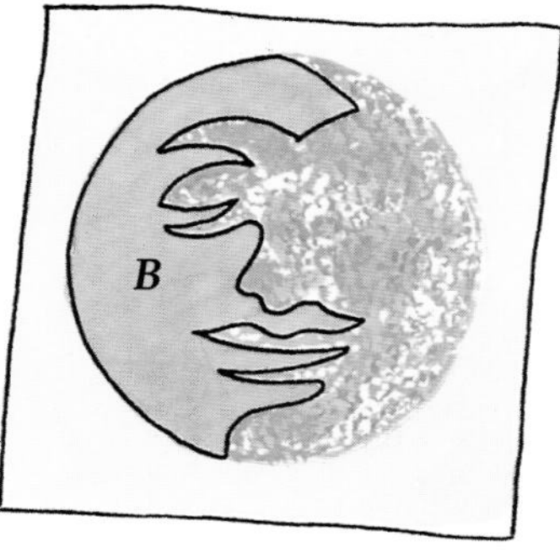

10. Print the moon's face in the same way as you printed the sun, but print side **B** onto the left-hand side of the circle.

11. Print stars in the spaces. Follow the manufacturer's instructions for making the paint permanent.

Hearts and squares

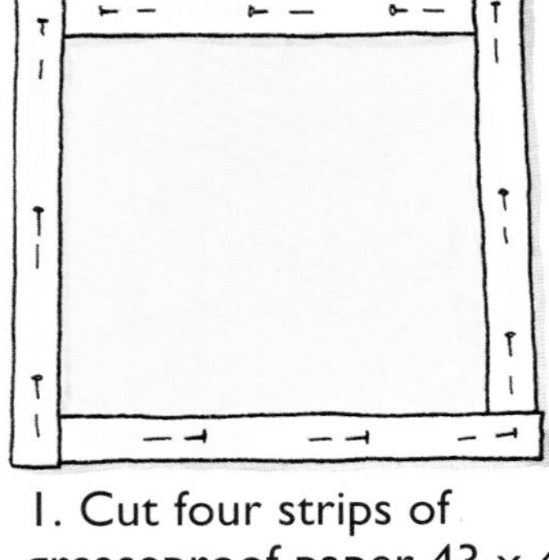

This project shows you how to print a piece of fabric large enough to cover a 40cm (16in) cushion. (See page 32 for how to make a cushion.) If you print with fabric paint, rather than acrylic paint, make sure that you follow the manufacturer's instructions for making the paint permanent.

You will need: 43cm (17in) square of cotton fabric; pencil; ruler; scissors; knitting yarn (not too fine); pins; tape; 11cm (4½in) square cereal box cardboard; greaseproof or tracing paper; paper; rag; fabric paint or acrylic paint; clean scrap paper; sponge cleaning cloth; old spoon; craft knife; potato.

1. Cut four strips of greaseproof paper 43 x 4cm (17 x 1½in). Pin around the fabric, matching the edges.

14cm(5½in)

Make a mark at both sides of the square.

2. Cut four more strips 17 x 2½cm (43 x 1in). Mark 14cm (5½in) from the top edge. Pin on a strip below the marks.

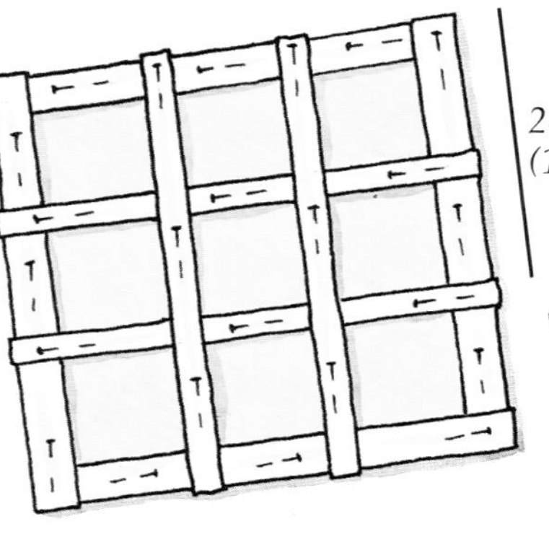

26.5cm (10½ in)

3. Pin another strip 26.5cm (10½in) from the top. Turn the fabric around and repeat so the strips cross each other.

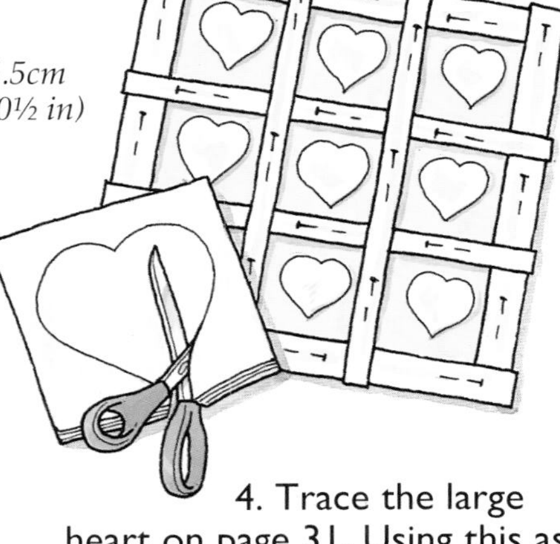

4. Trace the large heart on page 31. Using this as a pattern, cut out nine hearts. Lay one in each square.

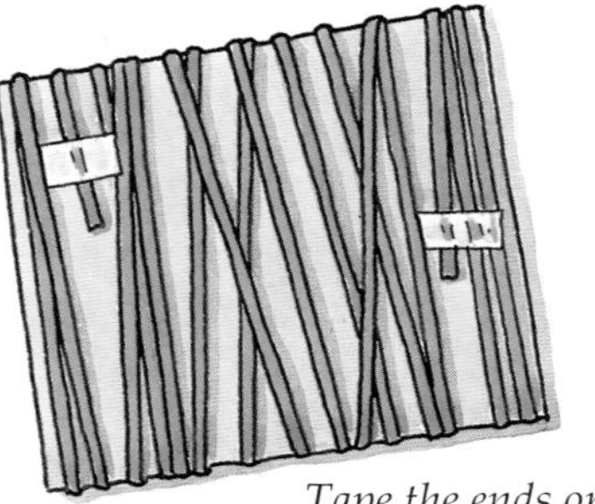

Tape the ends on the same side.

5. Tape one end of the yarn to the cardboard square. Wind all over in a criss-cross pattern until it is covered.

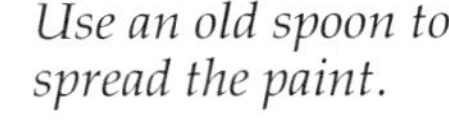

Use an old spoon to spread the paint.

6. Wet the sponge and squeeze it almost dry. Put it on newspaper and spread on paint with the back of a spoon.

7. Press the yarn, tape-side up, on the paint. Lay it over a square. Put paper over it and rub. Repeat for each square.

8. Trace and cut out the medium heart on page 31. Pin it onto a cut potato and use it as a pattern (see page 3).

If you print on a bag, push a big piece of cardboard inside before you begin. This helps to keep it flat and stops the paint from seeping through to the back.

9. Print a heart with the potato in each heart space. Leave to dry then remove all the pins and strips of paper.

10. Trace and cut out the small heart. Pin it onto a cut potato. Cut it out and print it between the squares.

The letters on the bag were printed with a potato. Make sure you cut them out back to front as they print in reverse.

Leaves, corks and bottle tops

Try printing with all kinds of things which you can find around your house and garden. **You will need**: paint; sponge cleaning cloth; newspaper; scrap paper; small decorator's paintbrush; a variety of leaves (try to find some leaves with unusual shapes or with strong vein patterns on their underside).

Leaf prints

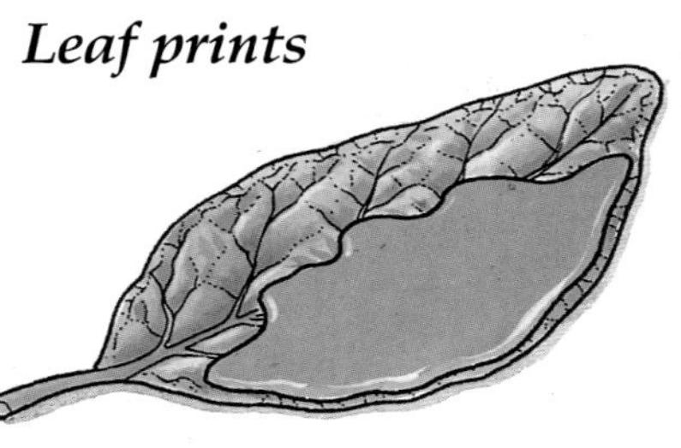

1. Painting from the middle of the leaf to the edge, cover the underside of a leaf with paint. Try to get an even layer which isn't too thick.

2. Carefully lay the leaf, paint-side down onto your paper. Lay scrap paper over the top and press lightly with the palm of your hand.

3. Lift off the scrap paper carefully and then peel off the leaf. If you need to, slip the tip of a knife under the edge of the leaf to help you lift it.

4. For a more delicate print, print the leaf again without adding any more paint. You can usually do three or four prints in this way.

Corks and bottle tops

Spread some paint onto a sponge cloth (see page 2). Dab the end of your object into the paint, then press it into your paper or fabric.

A cork prints a solid circle.

A screw head prints a circle with a line through it.

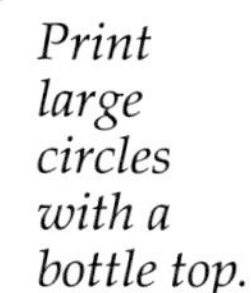

Print large circles with a bottle top.

Print small circles with a pen lid.

Rows

Do a print on scrap paper.

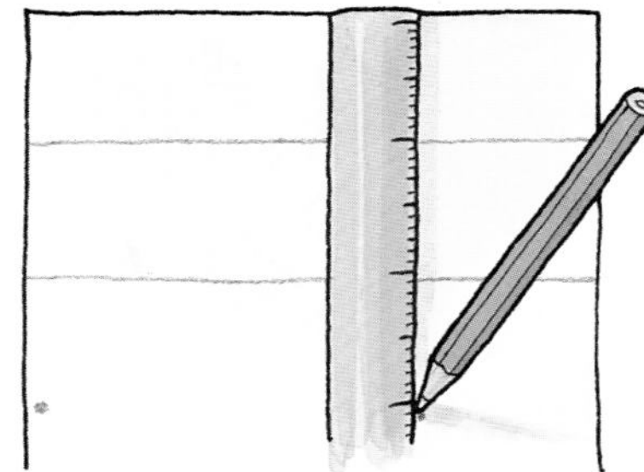

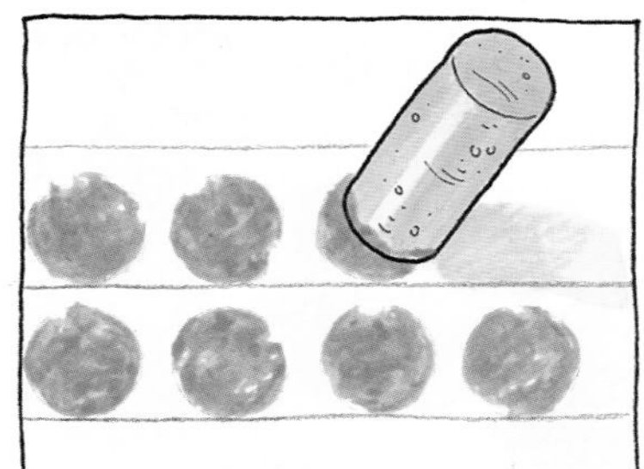

1. Measure the height of your print and add on 1cm (½in). Measure and mark this height with a pencil in several places along the top of your paper.

2. Using a ruler, join the dots with a faint pencil line. Measure another row of dots below the line you have drawn. Continue doing this down your paper.

3. Print each shape with the bottom of it just above the line you have drawn. Rub out all the lines with an eraser when your prints have dried.

Circles

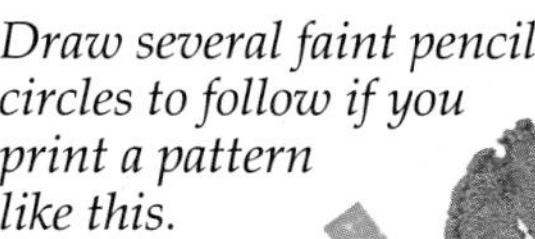

Draw several faint pencil circles to follow if you print a pattern like this.

1. Draw a circle around a mug or a saucer, or use a pair of compasses. Do a print at the top and the bottom of the circle, then at each side.

2. Fill in the gaps between the shapes you have already printed. Add more circles of prints inside this one if you want to.

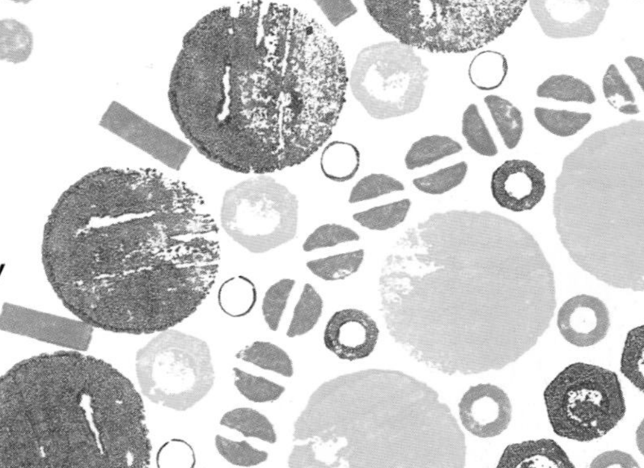

Rubber stamps

You can print complicated designs by cutting a simple pattern into an ordinary eraser. Be extra careful when cutting into one with a sharp craft knife.

You will need: one or more clean erasers; sharp craft knife; ruler; felt-tip pen; a toothpick or a mapping pin; acrylic paint; sponge cleaning cloth; kitchen paper towels.

Print on bright paper as well as white.

Triangle print

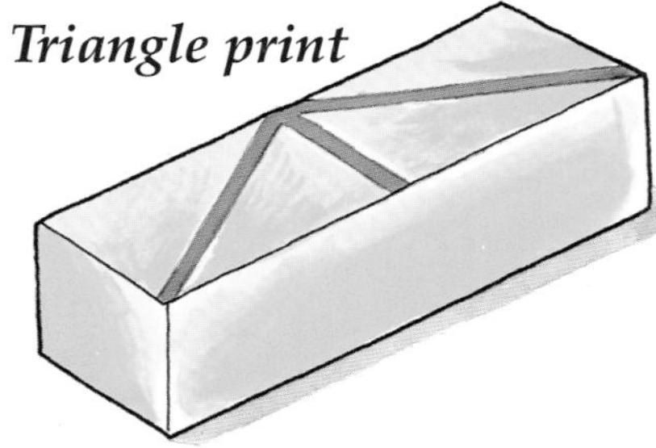

1. Mark the middle of the long edges of the eraser. Join the marks. Add the diagonal lines as shown, using a ruler.

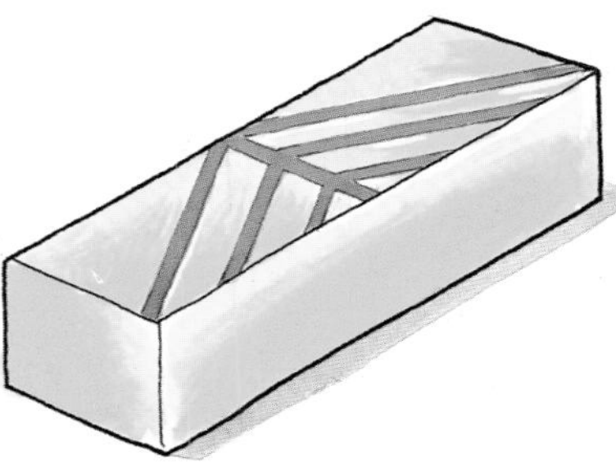

2. Using the middle line as a guide, add diagonal lines to make two more triangles. Try to space them evenly.

Carefully cut along the edges of the pen line.

3. With your craft knife at an angle, make a clean cut, about 3mm ($^1/_{10}$in) deep, along one side of the diagonal lines.

Repeat your print lots of times to make a pattern. *See page 23 to find out how to print even rows.*

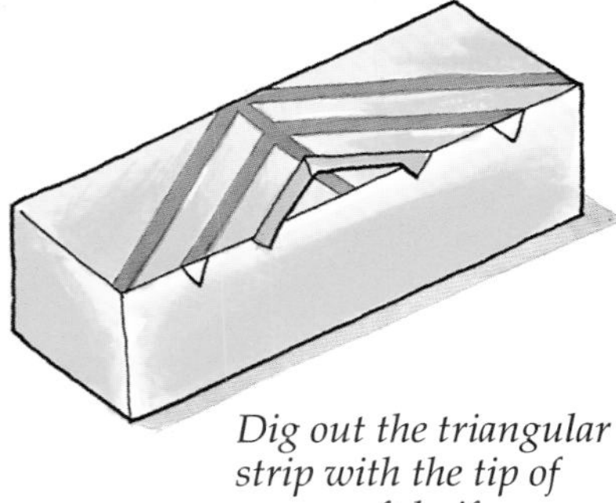

Dig out the triangular strip with the tip of your craft knife.

4. Cut at a slant along the other side of the line so that the cuts meet at the bottom. Repeat on the other side.

The shapes which are left are the shapes which will print.

5. Cut the other triangle in the same way. Slice down through the eraser along the edge of the larger triangle.

More patterns

You can experiment by cutting different shapes into your eraser to build up other printed patterns. You could also cut into the side and end of your eraser. Remember the pattern will be reversed when it's printed.

These lines were cut in a large square eraser.

Lines and triangles make an interesting pattern when they're printed in rows.

This pattern was printed with the eraser shown in the instructions.

Test your prints before you start your pattern.

Try printing simple lines with another eraser.

Try cutting lines at different angles into your eraser.

Use a piece of a toothpick instead of pin if you don't have one.

6. Make sure the channels you have cut are clear of any pieces of eraser. Turn it over and push in the mapping pin.

You don't need to put paint all over the cloth.

7. Wet the sponge cloth. Squeeze out as much water as you can so that it's almost dry. Spread paint onto the cloth.

Don't press too hard or some paint may seep out around the edges.

8. Press the eraser into the paint a few times, then test it. Press it in the paint every time you make a print.

Flour paste batik

You will need: fabric; large potato; cookie cutter; sharp knife; blunt knife; small bowl; two tablespoons of flour; two tablespoons of water; piece of sponge; fabric paints; newspaper; masking tape. Make sure your fabric is washed and ironed before you begin. You need to iron most types of fabric paint to make it permanent, so make sure you use a type of fabric which can be ironed.

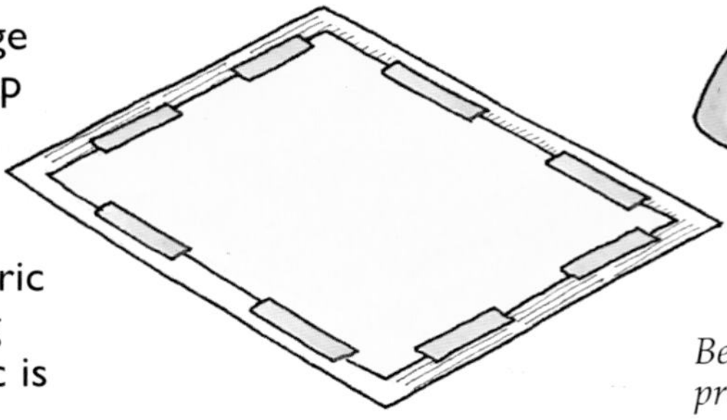

1. Lay the ironed fabric onto a flat surface over newspaper. Smooth out the fabric then tape it down in several places around the edge.

Be very careful as you press the potato down.

2. Cut the potato in half. Lay the cookie cutter sharp edge up and press half of the potato onto it. This makes it easier to hold as you print.

You could print in rows with more than one cookie cutter. Press it into the spare half of the potato.

If the lines are too thin, print over the shape again.

The print should leave a clear outline.

3. Mix the flour and water in the bowl until it becomes like glue. Dip the cutter in and shake off any drops. Try your print on paper.

4. To get a clear printed outline, you may need to add more flour to make the paste a little thicker, or some water to make it runnier.

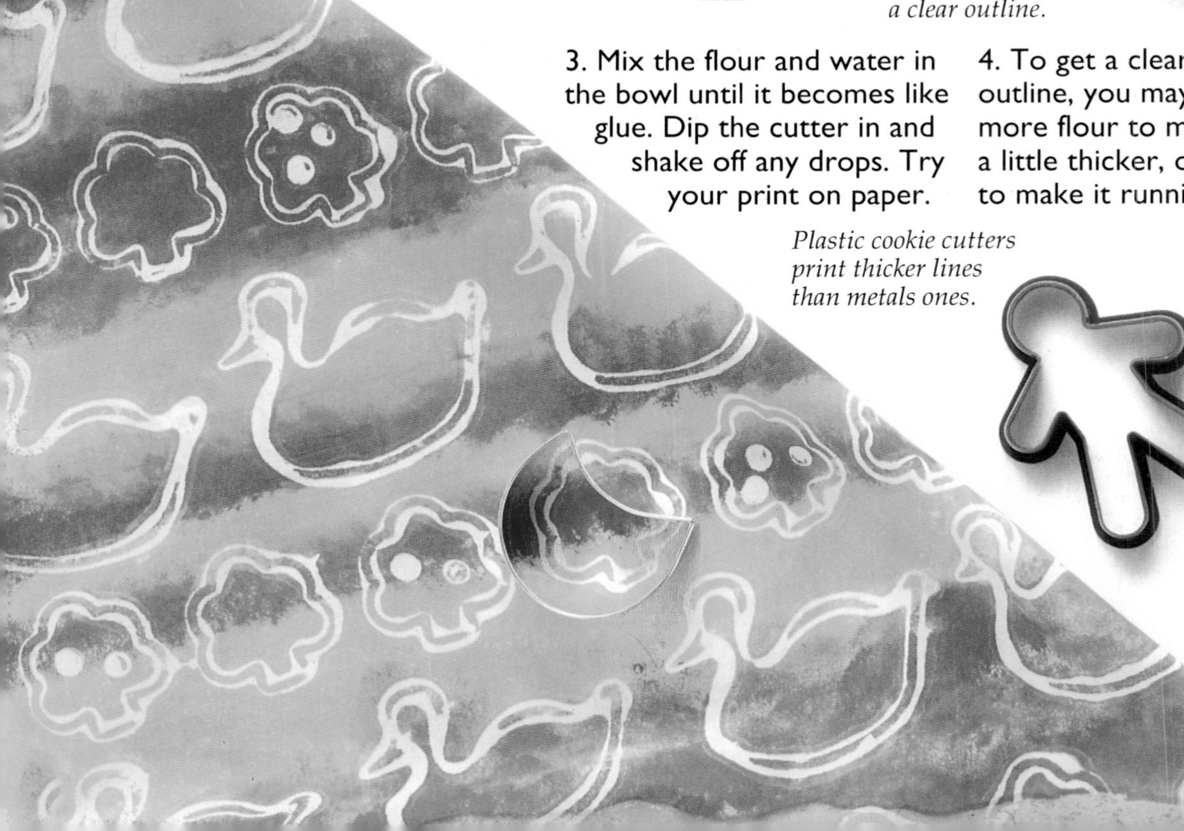

Plastic cookie cutters print thicker lines than metals ones.

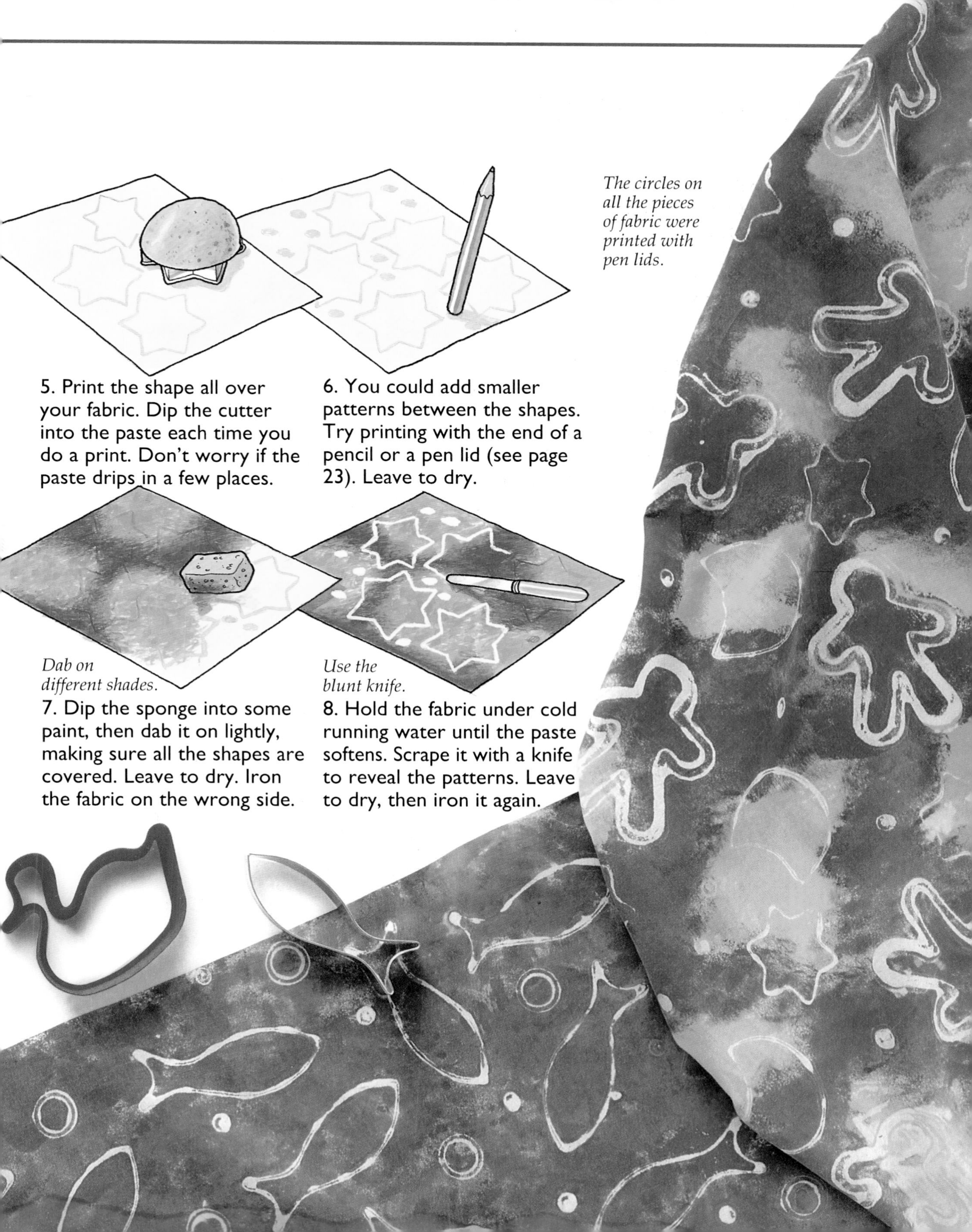

5. Print the shape all over your fabric. Dip the cutter into the paste each time you do a print. Don't worry if the paste drips in a few places.

6. You could add smaller patterns between the shapes. Try printing with the end of a pencil or a pen lid (see page 23). Leave to dry.

Dab on different shades.

7. Dip the sponge into some paint, then dab it on lightly, making sure all the shapes are covered. Leave to dry. Iron the fabric on the wrong side.

Use the blunt knife.

8. Hold the fabric under cold running water until the paste softens. Scrape it with a knife to reveal the patterns. Leave to dry, then iron it again.

The circles on all the pieces of fabric were printed with pen lids.

Lots more prints

Food tray prints

Cut out a shape from the patterned base of a food processing tray. Dip a small decorator's paintbrush into some paint. Dab it onto newspaper then paint the patterned side of your shape. Put it paint-side down and lay scrap paper over the top. Rub firmly with your hand. Peel the shape off carefully and add more paint.

Cut out large bold, simple shapes.

Use a craft knife or sharp scissors to cut out your shapes.

Corrugated cardboard

This cardboard gives you a textured print. Cut out shapes with a craft knife. If you print a letter shape, make sure that you cut it out back to front as it will print in reverse. Paint the shape and put it paint-side down onto your paper. Lay a piece of scrap paper over the back and rub it lightly.

If you want to print a letter draw it and cut it out back to front as it will print in reverse.

Cardboard prints

Dip the edge of a piece of cardboard into paint on a plate or sponge cloth, then print it. You can bend thin cardboard into all kinds of patterns or shapes. Hold it with both hands as you print.

For a fish, bend a piece of cardboard into a pear shape.

Add a V shape tail.

See page 5 for how to print a sea anemone.

Pipe cleaner prints

You can bend pipe cleaners into all kinds of shapes. Use an old pair of scissors if you want to cut them. Paint one side of your pipe cleaner shape, then lay it carefully paint-side down onto your paper. Lay a piece of thin cardboard on top and press lightly. Add more paint before printing again. Wipe the cardboard clean each time you print.

Rainbow shapes

Put several shades of paint onto newspaper in a patch, roughly the shape of a cookie cutter. Dip the cutter into the paint and print.

For identical prints dip it in the paint the same way each time.

Templates

Sun, moon and stars
pages 18-19

Fish for roller
print T-shirt
pages 12-13
Potato print hearts
pages 20-21
Juggling frog
pages 10-11
Lilypad for juggling
pages 10-11
Fish for roller print T-shirt
pages 12-13

Cushions and stitches

Making a cushion

You could print any of the designs in this book onto fabric and then make it into a cushion. To find out the size to cut your fabric, measure your cushion pad and add 3cm (1in) to each side. Cut two pieces of fabric to this size. **You will need:** cushion pad; needle; thread; pins; two pieces of washed and ironed cotton fabric.

Print your fabric and iron it before you start.

1. Pin the printed square, with the print inside, to the other piece of fabric. Pin 1.5cm (½in) from the edge.

2. Join the pieces by sewing 1.5cm (½in) from the edge with long tacking stitches (see below). Remove the pins.

3. Backstitch (see below) along three sides. Remove the tacking stitches, then turn the cover the right side out.

4. Push the cushion inside. Turn the open edges in 1.5cm (½in). Pin them together. Sew over the edges neatly.

Tacking stitch

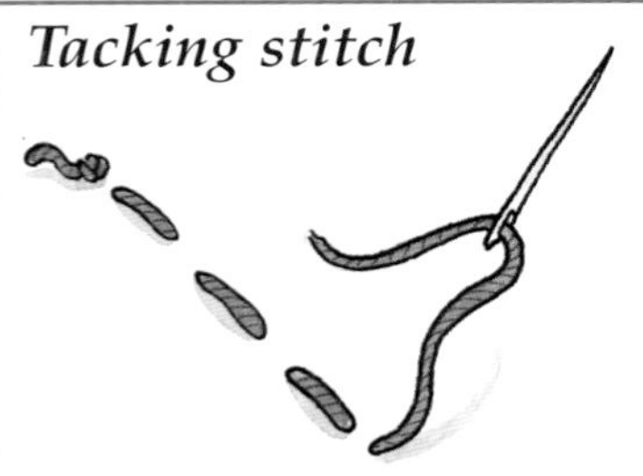

Tie a knot in one end of your thread. Sew in and out with long stitches about 1cm (½in) apart.

Backstitch

Tie a knot in one end before you start.

1. Make one stitch, then bring the needle up about 3mm (⅛in) away from it.

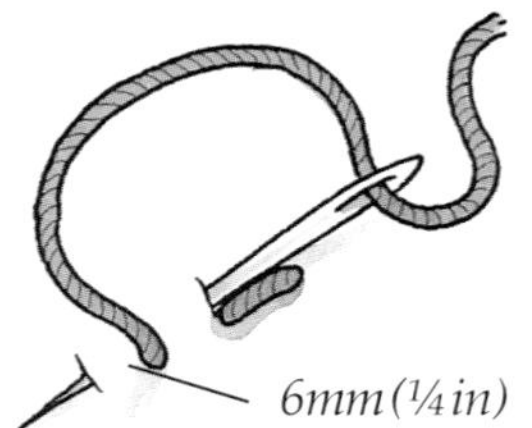

2. Put the needle in at the end of the stitch. Bring it up again 6mm (¼in) away.

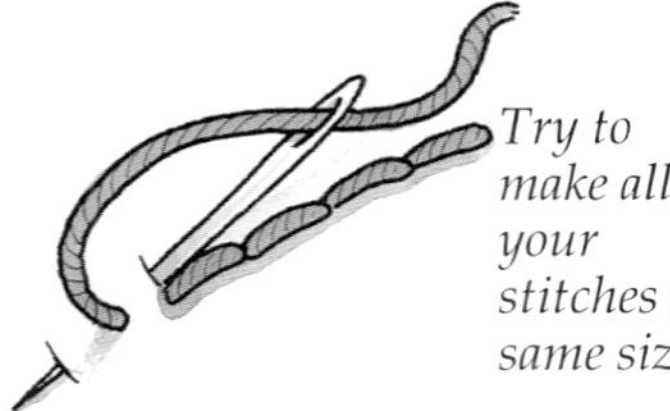

Try to make all your stitches the same size.

3. Continue in this way to make a neat line of continuous backstitches.

UE. First published in America in August 1996. Printed in Portugal.